KU-797-238

Chapter One

Little Bear lived with her dad at weekends. They always had lots of fun.

They played cool games like Monster Chase and Dad-is-a-Big-Climbing-Frame.

He helped her make brilliant dens and told funny jokes. He baked the best honey cookies.

But then, one Saturday...
"Play with me, Dad!" cried Little
Bear. "Let's play Puddle-Jumping.
Let's have a honey-eating race. Let's
go swimming in the Blue Lake!"

"Not now, sweetie," said her dad. "I've got some work to do on my computer, but I'll be finished soon." He sat down at his desk and started typing.

Chapter Two

Little Bear sighed.
She crawled under his desk to wait.
She waited…
And she waited…

"Is it soon yet, Dad?" she called up.
"Not yet," said her dad, typing faster
on his computer keyboard.

TAP,
TAP,
TAP...

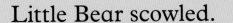

Little Bear scowled.
Waiting was SO boring.
Her dad was taking ages with his work,
and there was no one to play with.
She rolled over onto her tummy with
a huff.

Now her nose was right by her dad's
big paws.
Up close, his paws smelled of mud.
His claws looked very hard and shiny.

Little Bear had an idea for a game!
She pretended his claws were a
computer keyboard.
She typed on his claws...

TAP,
TAP,
TAP...

She giggled. It was fun.
But then: "Will you *please* stop tickling
my paws, Little Bear," snapped her dad.
"I'm busy."

Chapter Three

"Oh, but Dad…" moaned Little Bear. "I'm bored!"

"You'll just have to wait a bit longer," he said.

"I'm too thirsty to wait," said Little Bear.
Her dad sighed. He got up and fetched
her a glass of honey fizz.

"Thank you. But now I'm VERY
hungry," said Little Bear.
So her dad got up again and made her
a honey sandwich.

"Thank you. But now my ears feel hot," whined Little Bear. "And my fur hurts... and my teeth itch."

"Right, that's quite *enough*, Little Bear,"
growled her dad. "Please go and wait
in your room while I finish my work."
Little Bear scowled and ran to her room.

She rolled into a ball on the floor.
Her dad was being grumpy. He told
her off. It wasn't fair!

"Baddy Daddy," she muttered into the rug. "I want to go to my mum's now." She pretended to cry. But her dad didn't come.

Chapter Four

After a very, *very* long wait – it felt like a whole *year* – Little Bear heard heavy footsteps.

Her dad was coming along the corridor. But she still felt cross with him.

So, as quick as she could, Little Bear
did a roly-poly across her floor and
hid under her bed.

She heard her dad come into her room.
He was looking for her.

Little Bear held her breath and stayed very quiet.
Then, suddenly... **"BOO!"**

Her dad's big, furry nose appeared under the bed.

"I found you," he said. "I've finished my work now. Want to play?"

"No, sorry, I'm too busy," said Little Bear, turning away to face the wall.

"Okay," said her dad. "I'll wait."
He squashed under the bed next to her.

And he waited...

And he waited...

Then he pretended to type on her claws.

TAP,

TAP,

TAP...

"Please stop tickling my paws, Dad,"
said Little Bear. "I'm busy!"

But she couldn't help smiling. He was being too funny. She started giggling. "Okay, Dad, I've finished being busy now," she said. "Let's go and PLAY!"

Chapter Five

Little Bear and her dad went out into the woods.

It was a lovely day. The sun was shining through the leaves.

Little Bear held her dad's big paw and
skipped and sang.
They played Monster Chase and jumped
over muddy puddles.

They had a tree-climbing race and a
scary-growling competition.

They swam in the Blue Lake.

Then they had a picnic feast with honey cookies and honey ice cream for pudding.

On the way home, her dad carried
her on his shoulders.
She felt as high as the birds.

"See, Little Bear, it was a long wait, but did you have fun in the end?" asked her dad.
"Yes, I DID," cried Little Bear.

PILLGWENLLY

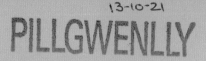

She hugged his head and kissed both
his furry ears.
Then she threw her paws in the air
and shouted into the tree tops:
"I LOVE my Daddy Bear!"